Defoe
Abbott
Marx
Hardy
Montaigne
Machiavelli
Chesterton
Cooper
Emerson
Joyce
Austen
Hugo
Eliot
Grimm
Melville
Christie
Carroll
Haggard
Molière
Stoker
Wilde
Maupassant
Byron
Schiller
Engels
Garnett
Einstein
Fitzgerald
Hawthorne
Smith
Kafka
Goethe
Dostoyevsky
Hall
Cotton
Kipling
Doyle
Willis
Baum
Henry
Nietzsche
Leslie
Dumas
Flaubert
Turgenev
Balzac
Stockton
Vatsyayana
Crane
Burroughs
Verne
Curtis
Tocqueville
Gogol
Vinci
Whitman
Homer
Widger
Tolstoy
Busch
Darwin
Thoreau
Potter
Twain
Scott
Plato
Zola
Lawrence
Harte
Kant
Freud
Jowett
Stevenson
Dickens
Andersen
London
Descartes
Burton
Hesse
Poe
Aristotle
Wells
Cervantes
Voltaire
Hale
James
Hastings
Cooke
Bunner
Shakespeare
Richter
Chambers
da
Shaw
Irving
Doré
Chekhov
Wodehouse
Benedict
Alcott
Dante
Pushkin
Swift
Newton

tredition®

tredition was established in 2006 by Sandra Latusseck and Soenke Schulz. Based in Hamburg, Germany, tredition offers publishing solutions to authors and publishing houses, combined with world-wide distribution of printed and digital book content. tredition is uniquely positioned to enable authors and publishing houses to create books on their own terms and without conventional manu-facturing risks.

For more information please visit: www.tredition.com

TREDITION CLASSICS

This book is part of the TREDITION CLASSICS series. The creators of this series are united by passion for literature and driven by the intention of making all public domain books available in printed format again - worldwide. Most TREDITION CLASSICS titles have been out of print and off the bookstore shelves for decades. At tredition we believe that a great book never goes out of style and that its value is eternal. Several mostly non-profit literature projects provide content to tredition. To support their good work, tredition donates a portion of the proceeds from each sold copy. As a reader of a TREDITION CLASSICS book, you support our mission to save many of the amazing works of world literature from oblivion. See all available books at www.tredition.com.

 Project Gutenberg

The content for this book has been graciously provided by Project Gutenberg. Project Gutenberg is a non-profit organization founded by Michael Hart in 1971 at the University of Illinois. The mission of Project Gutenberg is simple: To encourage the creation and distribution of eBooks. Project Gutenberg is the first and largest collection of public domain eBooks.

May Day with the Muses

Robert Bloomfield

Imprint

This book is part of TREDITION CLASSICS

Author: Robert Bloomfield
Cover design: Buchgut, Berlin – Germany

Publisher: tredition GmbH, Hamburg - Germany
ISBN: 978-3-8424-6666-1

www.tredition.com
www.tredition.de

PREFACE.

I am of opinion that Prefaces are very useless things in cases like the present, where the Author must talk of himself, with little amusement to his readers. I have hesitated whether I should say any thing or nothing; but as it is the fashion to say something, I suppose I must comply. I am well aware that many readers will exclaim—"It is not the common practice of English baronets to remit half a year's rent to their tenants for poetry, or for any thing else." This may be very true; but I have found a character in the Rambler, No. 82, who made a very different bargain, and who says, "And as Alfred received the tribute of the Welsh in wolves' heads, I allowed my tenants to pay their rents in butterflies, till I had exhausted the papilionaceous tribe. I then directed them to the pursuit of other animals, and obtained, by this easy method, most of the grubs and insects which land, air, or water can supply.........I have, from my own ground, the longest blade of grass upon record, and once accepted, as a half year's rent for a field of wheat, an ear, containing more grains than had been seen before upon a single stem."

I hope my old Sir Ambrose stands in no need of defence from me or from any one; a man has a right to do what he likes with his own estate. The characters I have introduced as candidates may not come off so easily; a cluster of poets is not likely to be found in one village, and the following lines, written by my good friend T. Park. Esq. of Hampstead, are not only true, but beautifully true, and I cannot omit them.

WRITTEN IN THE ISLE OF THANET,

August, 1790.

The bard, who paints from rural plains,
  Must oft himself the void supply
Of damsels pure and artless swains,

Of innocence and industry:

For sad experience shows the heart
  Of human beings much the same;
Or polish'd by insidious art,
  Or rude as from the clod it came.

And he who roams the village round,
  Or strays amid the harvest sere,
Will hear, as now, too many a sound
  Quiet would never wish to hear.

The wrangling rustics' loud abuse,
  The coarse, unfeeling, witless jest,
The threat obscene, the oath profuse,
  And all that cultured minds detest.

Hence let those Sylvan poets glean,
  Who picture life without a flaw;
Nature may form a perfect scene,
  But Fancy must the figures draw.

The word "fancy" connects itself with my very childhood, fifty years back. The fancy of those who wrote the songs which I was obliged to hear in infancy was a very inanimate and sleepy fancy. I could enumerate a dozen songs at least which all described sleeping shepherds and shepherdesses, and, in one instance, where they both went to sleep: this is not fair certainly; it is not even "watch and watch."

"As Damon and Phillis were keeping of sheep,
Being free from all care they retired to sleep," &c.

I must say, that if I understand any thing at all about keeping sheep, this is not the way to go to work with them. But such characters and such writings were fashionable, and fashion will beat common sense at any time.

With all the beauty and spirit of Cunningham's "Kate of Aberdeen," and some others, I never found any thing to strike my mind so forcibly as the last stanza of Dibdin's "Sailor's Journal" —

"At length, 'twas in the month of May,
  Our crew, it being lovely weather,
At three A.M. discovered day
  And England's chalky cliffs together!
At seven, up channel how we bore,
  Whilst hopes and fears rush'd o'er each fancy!
At twelve, I gaily jump'd on shore,
  And to my throbbing heart press'd Nancy."

This, to my feelings, is a balm at all times; it is spirit, animation, and imagery, all at once.

I will plead no excuses for any thing which the reader may find in this little volume, but merely state, that I once met with a lady in London, who, though otherwise of strong mind and good information, would maintain that "it is impossible for a blind man to fall in love." I always thought her wrong, and the present tale of "Alfred and Jennet" is written to elucidate my side of the question.

I have been reported to be dead; but I can assure the reader that this, like many other reports, is not true. I have written these tales in anxiety, and in a wretched state of health; and if these formidable foes have not incapacitated me, but left me free to meet the public eye with any degree of credit, that degree of credit I am sure I shall gain.

I am, with remembrance of what is past,

Most respectfully,

ROBERT BLOOMFIELD.

Shefford, Bedfordshire,

April 10th, 1822.

MAY-DAY WITH THE MUSES.

THE INVITATION

O for the strength to paint my joy once more!
That joy I feel when Winter's reign is o'er;
When the dark despot lifts his hoary brow,
And seeks his polar-realm's eternal snow.
Though black November's fogs oppress my brain,
Shake every nerve, and struggling fancy chain;
Though time creeps o'er me with his palsied hand,
And frost-like bids the stream of passion stand,
And through his dry teeth sends a shivering blast,
And points to more than fifty winters past,
Why should I droop with heartless, aimless eye?
Friends start around, and all my phantoms fly,
And Hope, upsoaring with expanded wing,
Unfolds a scroll, inscribed "Remember Spring."
Stay, sweet enchantress, charmer of my days,
And glance thy rainbow colours o'er my lays;
Be to poor Giles what thou hast ever been,
His heart's warm solace and his sovereign queen;
Dance with his rustics when the laugh runs high,
Live in the lover's heart, the maiden's eye;
Still be propitious when his feet shall stray
Beneath the bursting hawthorn-buds of May;
Warm every thought, and brighten every hour,
And let him feel thy presence and thy power.

SIR AMBROSE HIGHAM, in his eightieth year,
With memory unimpair'd, and conscience clear,
His English heart untrammell'd, and full blown
His senatorial honours and renown,
Now, basking in his plenitude of fame,

Resolved, in concert with his noble dame,
To drive to town no more—no more by night
To meet in crowded courts a blaze of light,
In streets a roaring mob with flags unfurl'd,
And all the senseless discord of the world, —
But calmly wait the hour of his decay,
The broad bright sunset of his glorious day;
And where he first drew breath at last to fall,
Beneath the towering shades of Oakly Hall[A].

[Footnote A: The seat of Sir Ambrose is situated in the author's imagination only; the reader must build Oakly Hall where he pleases.]

Quick spread the news through hamlet, field, and farm,
The labourer wiped his brow and staid his arm;
'Twas news to him of more importance far
Than change of empires or the yells of war;
It breathed a hope which nothing could destroy,
Poor widows rose, and clapp'd their hands for joy,
Glad voices rang at every cottage door,
"Good old Sir Ambrose goes to town no more."
Well might the village bells the triumph sound,
Well might the voice of gladness ring around;
Where sickness raged, or want allied to shame,
Sure as the sun his well-timed succour came;
Food for the starving child, and warmth and wine
For age that totter'd in its last decline.
From him they shared the embers' social glow;
He fed the flame that glanced along the snow,
When winter drove his storms across the sky,
And pierced the bones of shrinking poverty.

Sir Ambrose loved the Muses, and would pay
Due honours even to the ploughman's lay;
Would cheer the feebler bard, and with the strong
Soar to the noblest energies of song;
Catch the rib-shaking laugh, or from his eye

Dash silently the tear of sympathy.
Happy old man! — with feelings such as these
The seasons all can charm, and trifles please;
And hence a sudden thought, a new-born whim,
Would shake his cup of pleasure to the brim,
Turn scoffs and doubts and obstacles aside,
And instant action follow like a tide.

Time past, he had on his paternal ground
With pride the latent sparks of genius found
In many a local ballad, many a tale,
As wild and brief as cowslips in the dale,
Though unrecorded as the gleams of light
That vanish in the quietness of night
"Why not," he cried, as from his couch he rose,
"To cheer my age, and sweeten my repose,
"Why not be just and generous in time,
"And bid my tenants pay their rents in rhyme?
"For one half year they shall. — A feast shall bring
"A crowd of merry faces in the spring; —
"Here, pens, boy, pens; I'll weigh the case no more,
"But write the summons: — go, go, shut the door.

"'All ye on Oakly manor dwelling,
'Farming, labouring, buying, selling,
'Neighbours! banish gloomy looks,
'My grey old steward shuts his books.
'Let not a thought of winter's rent
'Destroy one evening's merriment;
'I ask not gold, but tribute found
'Abundant on Parnassian ground.
'Choose, ye who boast the gift, your themes
'Of joy or pathos, tales or dreams,
'Choose each a theme; — but, harkye, bring
'No stupid ghost, no vulgar thing;
'Fairies, indeed, may wind their way,
'And sparkle through the brightest lay:
'I love their pranks, their favourite green,

'And, could the little sprites be seen,
'Were I a king, I'd sport with them,
'And dance beneath my diadem.
'But surely fancy need not brood
'O'er midnight darkness, crimes, and blood,
'In magic cave or monk's retreat,
'Whilst the bright world is at her feet;
'Whilst to her boundless range is given,
'By night, by day, the lights of heaven,
'And all they shine upon; whilst Love
'Still reigns the monarch of the grove,
'And real life before her lies
'In all its thousand, thousand dies.
'Then bring me nature, bring me sense,
'And joy shall be your recompense:
'On Old May-day I hope to see
'All happy:—leave the rest to me.
'A general feast shall cheer us all
'Upon the lawn that fronts the hall,
'With tents for shelter, laurel boughs
'And wreaths of every flower that blows.
'The months are wending fast away;
'Farewell,—remember Old May-day.'"

Surprise, and mirth, and gratitude, and jeers,
The clown's broad wonder, th' enthusiast's tears,
Fresh gleams of comfort on the brow of care,
The sectary's cold shrug, the miser's stare,
Were all excited, for the tidings flew
As quick as scandal the whole country through.
"Rent paid by rhymes at Oakly may be great,
"But rhymes for taxes would appal the state,"
Exclaim'd th' exciseman,—"and then tithes, alas!
"Why there, again, 'twill never come to pass."—
Thus all still ventured, as the whim inclined,
Remarks as various as the varying mind:
For here Sir Ambrose sent a challenge forth,
That claim'd a tribute due to sterling worth;

And all, whatever might their host regale,
Agreed to share the feast and drink his ale.

Now shot through many a heart a secret fire,
A new born spirit, an intense desire
For once to catch a spark of local fame,
And bear a poet's honourable name!
Already some aloft began to soar,
And some to think who never thought before;
But O, what numbers all their strength applied,
Then threw despairingly the task aside
With feign'd contempt, and vow'd they'd never tried.
Did dairy-wife neglect to turn her cheese,
Or idling miller lose the favouring breeze;
Did the young ploughman o'er the furrows stand,
Or stalking sower swing an empty hand,
One common sentence on their heads would fall,
'Twas Oakly banquet had bewitch'd them all.
Loud roar'd the winds of March, with whirling snow,
One brightening hour an April breeze would blow;
Now hail, now hoar-frost bent the flow'ret's head,
Now struggling beams their languid influence shed,
That scarce a cowering bird yet dared to sing
'Midst the wild changes of our island spring.
Yet, shall the Italian goatherd boasting cry,
"Poor Albion! when hadst thou so clear a sky!"
And deem that nature smiles for him alone;
Her renovated beauties all his own?
No:—let our April showers by night descend,
Noon's genial warmth with twilight stillness blend;
The broad Atlantic pour her pregnant breath,
And rouse the vegetable world from death;
Our island spring is rapture's self to me,
All I have seen, and all I wish to see.

Thus came the jovial day, no streaks of red
O'er the broad portal of the morn were spread,
But one high-sailing mist of dazzling white,

A screen of gossamer, a magic light,
Doom'd instantly, by simplest shepherd's ken,
To reign awhile, and be exhaled at ten.
O'er leaves, o'er blossoms, by his power restored,
Forth came the conquering sun and look'd abroad;
Millions of dew-drops fell, yet millions hung,
Like words of transport trembling on the tongue
Too strong for utt'rance: — Thus the infant boy,
With rosebud cheeks, and features tuned to joy,
Weeps while he struggles with restraint or pain,
But change the scene, and make him laugh again,
His heart rekindles, and his cheek appears
A thousand times more lovely through his tears.

From the first glimpse of day a busy scene
Was that high swelling lawn, that destined green,
Which shadowless expanded far and wide,
The mansion's ornament, the hamlet's pride;
To cheer, to order, to direct, contrive,
Even old Sir Ambrose had been up at five;
There his whole household labour'd in his view, —
But light is labour where the task is new.
Some wheel'd the turf to build a grassy throne
Round a huge thorn that spread his boughs alone,
Rough-rined and bold, as master of the place;
Five generations of the Higham race
Had pluck'd his flowers, and still he held his sway,
Waved his white head, and felt the breath of May.
Some from the green-house ranged exotics round,
To back in open day on English ground:
And 'midst them in a line of splendour drew
Long wreaths and garlands, gather'd in the dew.
Some spread the snowy canvas, propp'd on high
O'er shelter'd tables with their whole supply;
Some swung the biting scythe with merry face,
And cropp'd the daisies for a dancing space.
Some roll'd the mouldy barrel in his might,
From prison'd darkness into cheerful light,

And fenced him round with cans; and others bore
The creaking hamper with its costly store,
Well cork'd, well flavour'd, and well tax'd, that came
From Lusitanian mountains, dear to fame,
Whence GAMA steer'd, and led the conquering way
To eastern triumphs and the realms of day.
A thousand minor tasks fill'd every hour,
'Till the sun gain'd the zenith of his power,
When every path was throng'd with old and young,
And many a sky-lark in his strength upsprung
To bid them welcome.—Not a face was there
But for May-day at least had banish'd care;
No cringing looks, no pauper tales to tell,
No timid glance, they knew their host too well,—
Freedom was there, and joy in every eye:
Such scenes were England's boast in days gone by.

Beneath the thorn was good Sir Ambrose found,
His guests an ample crescent form'd around;
Nature's own carpet spread the space between,
Where blithe domestics plied in gold and green.
The venerable chaplain waved his wand,
And silence follow'd as he stretch'd his hand,
And with a trembling voice, and heart sincere,
Implored a blessing on th' abundant cheer.
Down sat the mingling throng, and shared a feast
With hearty welcomes given, by love increased;
A patriarch family, a close-link'd band,
True to their rural chieftain, heart and hand:
The deep carouse can never boast the bliss,
The animation of a scene like this.

At length the damask cloths were whisk'd away,
Like fluttering sails upon a summer's day;
The hey-day of enjoyment found repose;
The worthy baronet majestic rose;
They view'd him, while his ale was filling round,
The monarch of his own paternal ground.

His cup was full, and where the blossoms bow'd
Over his head, Sir Ambrose spoke aloud,
Nor stopp'd a dainty form or phrase to cull —
His heart elated, like his cup, was full: —
"Full be your hopes, and rich the crops that fall;
"Health to my neighbours, happiness to all."
Dull must that clown be, dull as winter's sleet,
Who would not instantly be on his feet:
An echoing health to mingling shouts gave place,
"Sir Ambrose Higham, and his noble race."

Avaunt, Formality! thou bloodless dame,
With dripping besom quenching nature's flame;
Thou cankerworm, who liv'st but to destroy,
And eat the very heart of social joy; —
Thou freezing mist round intellectual mirth,
Thou spell-bound vagabond of spurious birth,
Away! away! and let the sun shine clear,
And all the kindnesses of life appear.

With mild complacency, and smiling brow,
The host look'd round, and bade the goblets flow;
Yet curiously anxious to behold
Who first would pay in rhymes instead of gold;
Each eye inquiring through the ring was glanced
To see who dared the task, who first advanced;
That instant started Philip from the throng,
Philip, a farmer's son, well known for song, —
And, as the mingling whispers round him ran,
He humbly bow'd, and timidly began: —

THE DRUNKEN FATHER

Poor Ellen married Andrew Hall,
  Who dwells beside the moor,
Where yonder rose-tree shades the wall,
  And woodbines grace the door.

Who does not know how blest, how loved
  Were her mild laughing eyes
By every youth!—but Andrew proved
  Unworthy of his prize.

In tippling was his whole delight,
  Each sign-post barr'd his way;
He spent in muddy ale at night
  The wages of the day.

Though Ellen still had charms, was young,
  And he in manhood's prime,
She sad beside her cradle sung,
  And sigh'd away her time.

One cold bleak night, the stars were hid,
  In vain she wish'd him home;
Her children cried, half cheer'd, half chid,
  "O when will father come!"

'Till Caleb, nine years old, upsprung,
  And kick'd his stool aside,
And younger Mary round him clung,
  "I'll go, and you shall guide."

The children knew each inch of ground,
  Yet Ellen had her fears;
Light from the lantern glimmer'd round,
  And show'd her falling tears.

"Go by the mill and down the lane;
  "Return the same way home:
"Perhaps you'll meet him, give him light;
  "O how I *wish* he'd come."

Away they went, as close and true
  As lovers in the shade,
And Caleb swung his father's staff
  At every step he made.

The noisy mill-clack rattled on,
  They saw the water flow,
And leap in silvery foam along,
  Deep murmuring below.

"We'll soon be there," the hero said,
  "Come on, 'tis but a mile, —
"Here's where the cricket-match was play'd,
  "And here's the shady stile.

"How the light shines up every bough!
  "How strange the leaves appear!
"Hark! — What was that? — 'tis silent now,
  "Come, Mary, never fear."

The staring oxen breathed aloud,
  But never dream'd of harm;
A meteor glanced along the cloud
  That hung o'er Wood-Hill Farm.

Old Caesar bark'd and howl'd hard by,
  All else was still as death,
But Caleb was ashamed to cry,
  And Mary held her breath.

At length they spied a distant light,
  And heard a chorus brawl;
Wherever drunkards stopp'd at night,
  Why there was Andrew Hall.

The house was full, the landlord gay,
  The bar-maid shook her head,
And wish'd the boobies far away
  That kept her out of bed.

There Caleb enter'd, firm, but mild,
  And spoke in plaintive tone:—
"My mother could not leave the child,
  "So we are come alone."

E'en drunken Andrew felt the blow
  That innocence can give,
When its resistless accents flow
  To bid affection live.

"I'm coming, loves, I'm coming now,"—
  Then, shuffling o'er the floor,
Contrived to make his balance true,
  And led them from the door.

The plain broad path that brought him there
  By day, though faultless then,
Was up and down and narrow grown,
  Though wide enough for ten.

The stiles were wretchedly contrived,
  The stars were all at play,
And many a ditch had moved itself
  Exactly in his way.

But still conceit was uppermost,
  That stupid kind of pride:—
"Dost think I cannot see a post?
  "Dost think I want a guide?

"Why, Mary, how you twist and twirl!
  "Why dost not keep the track?
"I'll carry thee home safe, my girl,"—
  Then swung her on his back.

Poor Caleb muster'd all his wits
  To bear the light ahead,
As Andrew reel'd and stopp'd by fits,
  Or ran with thund'ring tread.

Exult, ye brutes, traduced and scorn'd,
  Though true to nature's plan;
Exult, ye bristled, and ye horn'd,
  When infants govern man.

Down to the mill-pool's dangerous brink
  The headlong party drove;
The boy alone had power to think,
  While Mary scream'd above.

"Stop!" Caleb cried, "you've lost the path;
  "The water's close before;
"I see it shine, 'tis very deep,—
  "Why, don't you hear it roar?"

And then in agony exclaim'd,
  "O where's my mother *now*?"
The Solomon of hops and malt
  Stopp'd short and made a bow:

His head was loose, his neck disjointed,
  It cost him little trouble;
But, to be stopp'd and disappointed,
  Poh! danger was a bubble.

Onward be stepp'd, the boy alert,
  Calling his courage forth,
Hung like a log on Andrew's skirt,
  And down he brought them both.

The tumbling lantern reach'd the stream,
  Its hissing light soon gone;
'Twas night, without a single gleam,
  And terror reign'd alone.

A general scream the miller heard,
  Then rubb'd his eyes and ran,
And soon his welcome light appear'd,
  As grumbling he began: —

"What have we here, and whereabouts?
  "Why what a hideous squall!
"Some drunken fool! I thought as much —
  "'Tis only Andrew Hall!

"Poor children!" tenderly he said,
  "But now the danger's past."
They thank'd him for his light and aid,
  And drew near home at last.

But who upon the misty path
  To meet them forward press'd?
'Twas Ellen, shivering, with a babe
  Close folded to her breast.

Said Andrew, "Now you're glad, I know,
  "To se-se-see us come; —
"But I have taken care of both,
  "And brought them bo-bo-both safe home."

With Andrew vex'd, of Mary proud,
  But prouder of her boy,
She kiss'd them both, and sobb'd aloud, —
  The children cried for joy.

But what a home at last they found!
  Of comforts all bereft;
The fire out, the last candle gone,
  And not one penny left!

But Caleb quick as light'ning flew,
  And raised a light instead;
And as the kindling brands he blew,
  His father snored in bed.

No brawling, boxing termagant
  Was Ellen, though offended;
Who ever knew a fault like this
  By violence amended?

No: — she was mild as April morn,
  And Andrew loved her too;
She rose at daybreak, though forlorn,
  To try what love could do.

And as her waking husband groan'd,
  And roll'd his burning head,
She spoke with all the power of truth,
  Down kneeling by his bed.

"Dear Andrew, hear me, — though distress'd
  "Almost too much to speak, —
"This infant starves upon my breast —
  "To scold I am too weak.

"I work, I spin, I toil all day,
  "Then leave my work to cry,
"And start with horror when I think
  "You wish to see me die.

"But *do* you wish it? can that bring
  "More comfort, or more joy?
"Look round the house, how destitute!
  "Look at your ragged boy!

"That boy should make a father proud,
  "If any feeling can;
"Then save your children, save your wife,
  "Your honour as a man.

"Hear me, for God's sake hear me now,
  "And act a father's part!"
The culprit bless'd her angel tongue,
  And clasp'd her to his heart;

And would have vow'd, and would have sworn,
  But Ellen kiss'd him dumb, —
"Exert your mind, vow to *yourself*,
  "And better days will come.

"I shall be well when you are kind,
  "And you'll be better too." —
"I'll drink no more," — he quick rejoin'd, —
  "Be't poison if I do."

From that bright day his plants, his flowers,
  His crops began to thrive,
And for three years has Andrew been
  The soberest man alive.

Soon as he ended, acclamations 'rose,
Endang'ring modesty and self-repose,
Till the good host his prudent counsel gave,
Then listen'd all, the flippant and the grave.
"Let not applauses vanity inspire,
"Deter humility, or damp desire;
"Neighbours we are, then let the stream run fair,
"And every couplet be as free as air;
"Be silent when each speaker claims his right,
"Enjoy the day as I enjoy the sight:
"They shall not class us with the knavish elves,
"Who banish shame, and criticise themselves."

Thenceforward converse flow'd with perfect ease,
Midst country wit, and rustic repartees.
One drank to Ellen, if such might be found,
And archly glanced at female faces round.
If one with tilted can began to bawl,
Another cried, "Remember Andrew Hall."

Then, multifarious topics, corn and hay,
Vestry intrigues, the rates they had to pay,
The thriving stock, the lands too wet, too dry,
And all that bears on fruitful husbandry,
Ran mingling through the crowd — a crowd that might,
Transferr'd to canvas, give the world delight;
A scene that WILKIE might have touch'd with pride —

The May-day banquet then had never died.

But who is he, uprisen, with eye so keen,
In garb of shining plush of grassy green—
Dogs climbing round him, eager for the start,
With ceaseless tail, and doubly beating heart?
A stranger, who from distant forests came,
The sturdy keeper of the Oakly game.
Short prelude made, he pointed o'er the hill,
And raised a voice that every ear might fill;
His heart was in his theme, and in the forest still.

THE FORESTER.

[Illustration.]

THE FORESTER.

Born in a dark wood's lonely dell,
  Where echoes roar'd, and tendrils curl'd
Round a low cot, like hermit's cell,
  Old Salcey Forest was my world.
I felt no bonds, no shackles then,
  For life in freedom was begun;
I gloried in th' exploits of men,
  And learn'd to lift my father's gun.

O what a joy it gave my heart!
  Wild as a woodbine up I grew;
Soon in his feats I bore a part,
  And counted all the game he slew.
I learn'd the wiles, the shifts, the calls,
  The language of each living thing;
I mark'd the hawk that darting falls,
  Or station'd spreads the trembling wing.

I mark'd the owl that silent flits,
  The hare that feeds at eventide,
The upright rabbit, when he sits
  And mocks you, ere he deigns to hide.
I heard the fox bark through the night,
  I saw the rooks depart at morn,
I saw the wild deer dancing light,
  And heard the hunter's cheering horn.

Mad with delight, I roam'd around
  From morn to eve throughout the year,
But still, midst all I sought or found,
  My favourites were the spotted deer.
The elegant, the branching brow,
  The doe's clean limbs and eyes of love;
The fawn as white as mountain snow,
  That glanced through fern and brier and grove.

One dark, autumnal, stormy day,
  The gale was up in all its might,
The roaring forest felt its sway,
  And clouds were scudding quick as light:
A ruthless crash, a hollow groan,
  Aroused each self-preserving start,
The kine in herds, the hare alone,
  And shagged colts that grazed apart.

Midst fears instinctive, wonder drew
  The boldest forward, gathering strength
As darkness lour'd, and whirlwinds blew,
  To where the ruin stretch'd his length.
The shadowing oak, the noblest stem
  That graced the forest's ample bound,
Had cast to earth his diadem;
  His fractured limbs had delved the ground.

He lay, and still to fancy groan'd;
  He lay like Alfred when he died —
Alfred, a king by Heaven enthroned,
  His age's wonder, England's pride!
Monarch of forests, great as good,
  Wise as the sage, — thou heart of steel!
Thy name shall rouse the patriot's blood
  As long as England's sons can feel.

From every lawn, and copse, and glade,
  The timid deer in squadrons came,
And circled round their fallen shade
  With all of language but its name.
Astonishment and dread withheld
  The fawn and doe of tender years,
But soon a triple circle swell'd,
  With rattling horns and twinkling ears.

Some in his root's deep cavern housed,
  And seem'd to learn, and muse, and teach,
Or on his topmost foliage browsed,
  That had for centuries mock'd their reach.
Winds in their wrath these limbs could crash,
  This strength, this symmetry could mar;
A people's wrath can monarchs dash
  From bigot throne or purple car.

When Fate's dread bolt in Clermont's bowers
  Provoked its million tears and sighs,
A nation wept its fallen flowers,
  Its blighted hopes, its darling prize.—
So mourn'd my antler'd friends awhile,
  So dark, so dread, the fateful day;
So mourn'd the herd that knew no guile,
  Then turn'd disconsolate away!

Who then of language will be proud?
  Who arrogate that gift of heaven?
To wild herds when they bellow loud,
  To all the forest-tribes 'tis given.
I've heard a note from dale or hill
  That lifted every head and eye;
I've heard a scream aloft, so shrill
  That terror seized on all that fly.

Empires may fall, and nations groan,
  Pride be thrown down, and power decay;
Dark bigotry may rear her throne,
  But science is the light of day.
Yet, while so low my lot is cast,
  Through wilds and forests let me range;
My joys shall pomp and power outlast—
  The voice of nature cannot change.

    * * * * *

A soberer feeling through the crowd he flung,
Clermont was uppermost on every tongue;
But who can live on unavailing sighs?
The inconsolable are not the wise.
Spirit, and youth, and worth, demand a tear—
That day was past, and sorrow was not here;
Sorrow the contest dared not but refuse
'Gainst Oakly's open cellar and the muse.

Sir Ambrose cast his eye along the line,
Where many a cheerful face began to shine,
And, fixing on his man, cried, loud and clear,
"What have you brought, John Armstrong? let us hear."
Forth stepp'd his shepherd;—scanty locks of grey
Edged round a hat that seem'd to mock decay;
Its loops, its bands, were from the purest fleece,
Spun on the hills in silence and in peace.
A staff he bore carved round with birds and flowers,
The hieroglyphics of his leisure hours;
And rough form'd animals of various name,
Not just like BEWICK'S, but they meant the same.
Nor these alone his whole attention drew,
He was a poet,—this Sir Ambrose knew,—
A strange one too;—and now had penn'd a lay,
Harmless and wild, and fitting for the day.
No tragic tale on stilts;—his mind had more
Of boundless frolic than of serious lore;—

Down went his hat, his shaggy friend close by
Dozed on the grass, yet watch'd his master's eye.

THE SHEPHERD'S DREAM:

OR, FAIRIES' MASQUERADE.

[Illustration]

THE SHEPHERD'S DREAM: OR, FAIRIES' MASQUERADE.

I had folded my flock, and my heart was o'erflowing,
I loiter'd beside the small lake on the heath;
The red sun, though down, left his drapery glowing,
And no sound was stirring, I heard not a breath:
I sat on the turf, but I meant not to sleep,
And gazed o'er that lake which for ever is new,
Where clouds over clouds appear'd anxious to peep
From this bright double sky with its pearl and its blue.

Forgetfulness, rather than slumber, it seem'd,
When in infinite thousands the fairies arose
All over the heath, and their tiny crests gleam'd
In mock'ry of soldiers, our friends and our foes.
There a stripling went forth, half a finger's length high,
And led a huge host to the north with a dash;
Silver birds upon poles went before their wild cry,
While the monarch look'd forward, adjusting his sash.

Soon after a terrible bonfire was seen,
The dwellings of fairies went down in their ire,
But from all I remember, I never could glean
Why the woodstack was burnt, or who set it on fire.
The flames seem'd to rise o'er a deluge of snow,
That buried its thousands, — the rest ran away;
For the hero had here overstrain'd his long bow,

Yet he honestly own'd the mishap of the day.

Then the fays of the north like a hailstorm came on,
And follow'd him down to the lake in a riot,
Where they found a large stone which they fix'd him upon,
And threaten'd, and coax'd him, and bade him be quiet.
He that couquer'd them all, was to conquer no more,
But the million beheld he could conquer alone;
After resting awhile, he leap'd boldly on shore,
When away ran a fay that had mounted his throne.

'Twas pleasant to see how they stared, how they scamper'd,
By furze-bush, by fern, by no obstacle stay'd,
And the few that held council, were terribly hamper'd,
For some were vindictive, and some were afraid.
I saw they were dress'd for a masquerade train,
Colour'd rags upon sticks they all brandish'd in view,
And of such idle things they seem'd mightily vain,
Though they nothing display'd but a bird split in two.

Then out rush'd the stripling in battle array,
And both sides determined to fight and to maul:
Death rattled his jawbones to see such a fray,
And glory personified laugh'd at them all.
Here he fail'd, — hence he fled, with a few for his sake,
And leap'd into a cockle-shell floating hard by;
It sail'd to an isle in the midst of the lake,
Where they mock'd fallen greatness, and left him to die.

Meanwhile the north fairies stood round in a ring,
Supporting his rival on guns and on spears,
Who, though not a soldier, was robed like a king;
Yet some were exulting, and some were in tears.
A lily triumphantly floated above,
The crowd press'd, and wrangling was heard through the whole;
Some soldiers look'd surly, some citizens strove

To hoist the old nightcap on liberty's pole.

But methought in my dream some bewail'd him that fell,
And liked not his victors so gallant, so clever,
Till a fairy stepp'd forward, and blew through a shell,
"Bear misfortune with firmness, you'll triumph for ever."
I woke at the sound, all in silence, alone,
The moor-hens were floating like specks on a glass,
The dun clouds were spreading, the vision was gone,
And my dog scamper'd round 'midst the dew on the grass.

I took up my staff, as a knight would his lance,
And said, "Here 's my sceptre, my baton, my spear,
And there's my prime minister far in advance,
Who serves me with truth for his food by the year."
So I slept without care till the dawning of day,
Then trimm'd up my woodbines and whistled amain;
My minister heard as he bounded away,
And we led forth our sheep to their pastures again.

Scorch'd by the shadeless sun on Indian plains,
Mellow'd by age, by wants, and toils, and pains,
Those toils still lengthen'd when he reach'd that shore
Where Spain's bright mountains heard the cannons roar,
A pension'd veteran, doom'd no more to roam,
With glowing heart thus sung the joys of home.

THE SOLDIER'S HOME.

[Illustration.]

THE SOLDIER'S HOME.

My untried muse shall no high tone assume,
Nor strut in arms;—farewell my cap and plume:
Brief be my verse, a task within my power,
I tell my feelings in one happy hour;
But what an hour was that! when from the main
I reach'd this lovely valley once again!
A glorious harvest fill'd my eager sight,
Half shock'd, half waving in a flood of light;
On that poor cottage roof where I was born
The sun look'd down as in life's early morn.
I gazed around, but not a soul appear'd,
I listen'd on the threshold, nothing heard;
I call'd my father thrice, but no one came;
It was not fear or grief that shook my frame,
But an o'erpowering sense of peace and home,
Of toils gone by, perhaps of joys to come.
The door invitingly stood open wide,
I shook my dust, and set my staff aside.
How sweet it was to breathe that cooler air,
And take possession of my father's chair!
Beneath my elbow, on the solid frame,
Appear'd the rough initials of my name,
Cut forty years before!—the same old clock
Struck the same bell, and gave my heart a shock
I never can forget. A short breeze sprung,
And while a sigh was trembling on my tongue,
Caught the old dangling almanacks behind,
And up they flew, like banners in the wind;
Then gently, singly, down, down, down, they went,

And told of twenty years that I had spent
Far from my native land: — that instant came
A robin on the threshold; though so tame,
At first he look'd distrustful, almost shy,
And cast on me his coal-black stedfast eye,
And seem'd to say (past friendship to renew)
"Ah ha! old worn-out soldier, is it you?"
Through the room ranged the imprison'd humble bee,
And bomb'd, and bounced, and straggled to be free,
Dashing against the panes with sullen roar,
That threw their diamond sunlight on the floor;
That floor, clean sanded, where my fancy stray'd
O'er undulating waves the broom had made,
Reminding me of those of hideous forms
That met us as we pass'd the *Cape of Storms*,
Where high and loud they break, and peace comes never;
They roll and foam, and roll and foam for ever.
But *here* was peace, that peace which home can yield;
The grasshopper, the partridge in the field,
And ticking clock, were all at once become
The substitutes for clarion, fife, and drum.
While thus I mused, still gazing, gazing still
On beds of moss that spread the window sill,
I deem'd no moss my eyes had ever seen
Had been so lovely, brilliant, fresh, and green,
And guess'd some infant hand had placed it there,
And prized its hue, so exquisite, so rare.
Feelings on feelings mingling, doubling rose,
My heart felt every thing but calm repose;
I could not reckon minutes, hours, nor years,
But rose at once, and bursted into tears;
Then, like a fool, confused, sat down again,
And thought upon the past with shame and pain;
I raved at war and all its horrid cost,
And glory's quagmire, where the brave are lost.
On carnage, fire, and plunder, long I mused,
And cursed the murdering weapons I had used.

Two shadows then I saw, two voices heard,
One bespoke age, and one a child's appear'd.—
In stepp'd my father with convulsive start,
And in an instant clasp'd me to his heart.
Close by him stood a little blue-eyed maid,
And, stooping to the child, the old man said,
"Come hither, Nancy, kiss me once again,
This is your uncle Charles, come home from Spain."
The child approach'd, and with her fingers light,
Stroked my old eyes, almost deprived of sight.—
But why thus spin my tale, thus tedious be?
Happy old Soldier! what's the world to me?

   * * * * *

Change is essential to the youthful heart,
It cannot bound, it cannot act its part
To one monotonous delight a slave;
E'en the proud poet's lines become its grave:
By innate buoyancy, by passion led,
It acts instinctively, it will be fed.

A troop of country lasses paced the green,
Tired of their seats, and anxious to be seen;
They pass'd Sir Ambrose, turn'd, and pass'd again,
Some lightly tripp'd, to make their meaning plain:
The old man knew it well, the thoughts of youth
Came o'er his mind like consciousness of truth,
Or like a sunbeam through a lowering sky,
It gave him youth again, and ecstacy;
He joy'd to see them in this favourite spot,
Who of fourscore, or fifty score, would not?
He wink'd, he nodded, and then raised his hand,—
'Twas seen and answer'd by the Oakly band.
Forth leap'd the light of heart and light of heel,
E'en stiff limb'd age the kindling joy could feel.
They form'd, while yet the music started light;
The grass beneath their feet was short and bright,

Where thirty couple danced with all their might.
The Forester caught lasses one by one,
And twirl'd his glossy green against the sun;
The Shepherd threw his doublet on the ground,
And clapp'd his hands, and many a partner found:
His hat-loops bursted in the jocund fray,
And floated o'er his head like blooming May.
Behind his heels his dog was barking loud,
And threading all the mazes of the crowd;
And had he boasted one had wagg'd his tail,
And plainly said, "What can my master ail?"
To which the Shepherd, had he been more cool,
Had only said, "'Tis Oakly feast, you fool."

But where was Philip, he who danced so well?
Had he retired, had pleasure broke her spell?
No, he had yielded to a tend'rer bond,
He sat beside his own sick Rosamond,
Whose illness long deferr'd their wedding hour;
She wept, and seem'd a lily in a shower;
She wept to see him 'midst a crowd so gay,
For her sake lose the honours of the day.
But could a gentle youth be so unkind?
Would Philip dance, and leave his girl behind?
She in her bosom hid a written prize,
Inestimably rich in Philip's eyes;
The warm effusion of a heart that glow'd
With joy, with love, and hope by Heaven bestow'd.
He woo'd, he soothed, and every art assay'd,
To hush the scruples of the bashful maid,
Drawing, at length, against her weak command,
Reluctantly the treasure from her hand:
And would have read, but passion chain'd his tongue,
He turn'd aside, and down the ballad flung;
And paused so long from feeling and from shame,
That old Sir Ambrose halloo'd him by name:
"Bring it to me, my lad, and never fear,
"I never blamed true love, or scorn'd a tear;

"They well become us, e'en where branded most."
He came, and made a proxy of his host,
Who, as the dancers cooling join'd the throng,
Eyed the fair writer as he read her song.

ROSAMOND'S SONG OF HOPE.

Sweet Hope, so oft my childhood's friend,
  I will believe thee still,
For thou canst joy with sorrow blend,
  Where grief alone would kill.

When disappointments wrung my heart,
  Ill brook'd in tender years,
Thou, like a sun, perform'dst thy part,
  And dried my infant tears.

When late I wore the bloom of health,
  And love had bound me fast,
My buoyant heart would sigh by stealth
  For fear it might not last.

My sickness came, my bloom decay'd,
  But Philip still was by;
And thou, sweet Hope, so kindly said,
  "He'll weep if thou should'st die."

Thou told'st me too, that genial Spring
  Would bring me health again;
I feel its power, but cannot sing
  Its glories yet for pain.

But thou canst still my heart inspire,
  And Heaven can strength renew;
I feel thy presence, holy fire!
  My Philip will be true.

* * * * *

All eyes were turn'd, all hearts with pity glow'd,
The maid stood trembling, and the lover bow'd
As rose around them, while she dried her tears,
"Long life to Rosamond, and happy years!"

Scarce had the voices ceased, when forth there came
Another candidate for village fame:
By gratitude to Heaven, by honest pride,
Impell'd to rise and cast his doubts aside,
A sturdy yeoman, button'd to the throat,
Faced the whole ring, and shook his leathern coat.
"I have a tale of private life to tell,
"'Tis all of self and home, I know it well;
"In love and honour's cause I would be strong,
"Mine is a father's tale, perhaps too long,
"For fathers, when a duteous child's the theme,
"Can talk a summer's sun down, and then dream
"Of retrospective joys with hearts that glow
"With feelings such as parents only know."

ALFRED AND JENNET.

Yes, let me tell of Jennet, my last child;
In her the charms of all the rest ran wild,
And sprouted as they pleased. Still by my side,
I own she was my favourite, was my pride,
Since first she labour'd round my neck to twine,
Or clasp'd both little hands in one of mine:
And when the season broke, I've seen her bring
Lapfuls of flowers, and then the girl would sing
Whole songs, and halves, and bits, O, with such glee!
If playmates found a favourite, it was she.
Her lively spirit lifted her to joy;
To distance in the race a clumsy boy
Would raise the flush of conquest in her eye,
And all was dance, and laugh, and liberty.
Yet not hard-hearted, take me right, I beg,
The veriest romp that ever wagg'd a leg
Was Jennet; but when pity soothed her mind,
Prompt with her tears, and delicately kind.
The half-fledged nestling, rabbit, mouse, or dove,
By turns engaged her cares and infant love;
And many a one, at the last doubtful strife,
Warm'd in her bosom, started into life.

At thirteen she was all that Heaven could send,
My nurse, my faithful clerk, my lively friend;
Last at my pillow when I sunk to sleep,
First on my threshold soon as day could peep:
I heard her happy to her heart's desire,
With clanking pattens, and a roaring fire.

Then, having store of new-laid eggs to spare,
She fill'd her basket with the simple fare,

And weekly trudged (I think I see her still)
To sell them at yon house upon the hill.
Oft have I watch'd her as she stroll'd along,
Heard the gate bang, and heard her morning song;
And, as my warm ungovern'd feelings rose,
Said to myself, "Heaven bless her! there she goes."
Long would she tarry, and then dancing home,
Tell how the lady bade her oft'ner come,
And bade her talk and laugh without control;
For Jennet's voice was music to the soul,
My tale shall prove it:—For there dwelt a son,
An only child, and where there is but one,
Indulgence like a mildew reigns, from whence
Mischief may follow if that child wants sense.
But Alfred was a youth of noble mind,
With ardent passions, and with taste refined;
All that could please still courted heart and hand,
Music, joy, peace, and wealth, at his command;
Wealth, which his widow'd mother deem'd his own;
Except the poor, she lived for him alone.
Yet would she weep by stealth when he was near,
But check'd all sighs to spare his wounded ear;
For from his cradle he had never seen
Soul-cheering sunbeams, or wild nature's green.
But all life's blessings centre not in sight;
For Providence, that dealt him one long night,
Had given, in pity to the blooming boy,
Feelings more exquisitely tuned to joy.
Fond to excess was he of all that grew;
The morning blossom sprinkled o'er with dew,
Across his path, as if in playful freak,
Would dash his brow, and weep upon his cheek;
Each varying leaf that brush'd where'er he came,
Press'd to his rosy lip he call'd by name;
He grasp'd the saplings, measured every bough,
Inhaled the fragrance that the spring months throw
Profusely round, till his young heart confess'd
That all was beauty, and himself was bless'd.
Yet when he traced the wide extended plain,

Or clear brook side, he felt a transient pain;
The keen regret of goodness, void of pride,
To think he could not roam without a guide.

Who, guess ye, knew these scenes of home delight
Better than Jennet, bless'd with health and sight?
Whene'er she came, he from his sports would slide,
And catch her wild laugh, listening by her side;
Mount to the tell-tale clock with ardent spring,
And *feel* the passing hour, then fondly cling
To Jennet's arm, and tell how sweet the breath
Of bright May-mornings on the open heath;
Then off they started, rambling far and wide,
Like Cupid with a wood-nymph by his side.

Thus months and months roll'd on, the summer pass'd,
And the long darkness, and the winter blast,
Sever'd the pair; no flowery fields to roam,
Poor Alfred sought his music and his home.
What wonder then if inwardly he pined?
The anxious mother mark'd her stripling's mind
Gloomy and sad, yet striving to be gay
As the long tedious evenings pass'd away:
'Twas her delight fresh spirits to supply. —
My girl was sent for — just for company.

A tender governess my daughter found,
Her temper placid, her instruction sound;
Plain were her precepts, full of strength, their power
Was founded on the practice of the hour:
Theirs were the happy nights to peace resign'd,
With ample means to cheer th' unbended mind.
The Sacred History, or the volumes fraught
With tenderest sympathy, or towering thought,
The laughter-stirring tale, the moral lay,
All that brings dawning reason into day.
There Jennet learn'd by maps, through every land

To travel, and to name them at command;
Would tell how great their strength, their bounds how far,
And show where uncle Charles was in the war.
The globe she managed with a timid hand,
Told which was ocean, which was solid land,
And said, whate'er their diff'rent climates bore,
All still roll'd round, though that I knew before.

Thus grown familiar, and at perfect ease,
What could be Jennet's duty but to please?
Yet hitherto she kept, scarce knowing why,
One powerful charm reserved, and still was shy.
When Alfred from his grand-piano drew
Those heavenly sounds that seem'd for ever new,
She sat as if to sing would be a crime,
And only gazed with joy, and nodded time.
Till one snug evening, I myself was there,
The whispering lad inquired, behind my chair,
"Bowman, can Jennet sing?" "At home," said I,
"She sings from morn till night, and seems to fly
"From tune to tune, the sad, the wild, the merry,
"And moulds her lip to suit them like a cherry;
"She learn'd them here." — "O ho!" said he, "O ho!"
And rubb'd his hands, and stroked his forehead, so.
Then down he sat, sought out a tender strain,
Sung the first words, then struck the chords again;
"Come, Jennet, help me, you *must* know this song
"Which I have sung, and you have heard so long."
I mark'd the palpitation of her heart,
Yet she complied, and strove to take a part,
But faint and fluttering, swelling by degrees,
Ere self-composure gave that perfect ease,
The soul of song: — then, with triumphant glee,
Resting her idle work upon her knee,
Her little tongue soon fill'd the room around
With such a voluble and magic sound,
That, 'spite of all her pains to persevere,
She stopp'd to sigh, and wipe a starting tear;

Then roused herself for faults to make amends.
While Alfred trembled to his fingers' ends.

But when this storm of feeling sunk to rest,
Jennet, resuming, sung her very best,
And on the ear, with many a dying fall,
She pour'd th' enchanting "Harp of Tara's Hall."
Still Alfred hid his raptures from her view,
Still touch'd the keys, those raptures to renew,
And led her on to that sweet past'ral air,
The Highland Laddie with the yellow hair.
She caught the sound, and with the utmost ease
Bade nature's music triumph, sure to please:
Such truth, such warmth, such tenderness express'd,
That my old heart was dancing in my breast.
Upsprung the youth, "O Jennet, where's your hand?
"There's not another girl in all the land,
"If she could bring me empires, bring me sight,
"Could give me such unspeakable delight:
"You little baggage! not to tell before
"That you could sing; mind—you go home no more."

Thus I have seen her from my own fire-side
Attain the utmost summit of her pride;
For, from that singing hour, as time roll'd round,
At the great house my Jennet might be found,
And, while I watch'd her progress with delight,
She had a father's blessing every night,
And grew in knowledge at that moral school
Till I began to guess myself a fool.
Music! why she could play as well as he!
At least I thought so,—but we'll let that be:
She read the poets, grave and light, by turns,
And talk'd of Cowper's "Task," and Robin Burns;
Nay, read without a book, as I may say,
As much as some could with in half a day.
'Twas thus I found they pass'd their happy time,
In all their walks, when nature in her prime

Spread forth her scents and hues, and whisper'd love
And joy to every bird in every grove;
And though their colours could not meet his eye,
She pluck'd him flowers, then talk'd of poetry.

Once on a sunbright morning, 'twas in June,
I felt my spirits and my hopes in tune,
And idly rambled forth, as if t' explore
The little valley just before my door;
Down by yon dark green oak I found a seat
Beneath the clustering thorns, a snug retreat
For poets, as I deem'd, who often prize
Such holes and corners far from human eyes;
I mark'd young Alfred, led by Jennet, stray
Just to the spot, both chatting on their way:
They came behind me, I was still unseen;
He was the elder, Jennet was sixteen.
My heart misgave me, lest I should be deem'd
A prying listener, never much esteem'd,
But this fear soon subsided, and I said,
"I'll hear this blind lad and my little maid."
That instant down she pluck'd a woodbine wreath,
The loose leaves rattled on my head beneath;
This was for Alfred, which he seized with joy,
"O, thank you, Jennet," said the generous boy.
Much was their talk, which many a theme supplied,
As down they sat, for every blade was dried.

I would have skulk'd away, but dare not move,
"Besides," thought I, "they will not talk of love;"
But I was wrong, for Alfred, with a sigh,
A little tremulous, a little shy,
But, with the tenderest accents, ask'd his guide
A question which might touch both love and pride.
"This morning, Jennet, why did you delay,
"And talk to that strange clown upon your way,
"Our homespun gardener? how can you bear
"His screech-owl tones upon your perfect ear?

"I cannot like that man, yet know not why,
"He's surely quite as old again as I;
"He's ignorant, and cannot be your choice,
"And ugly too, I'm certain, by his voice,
"Besides, he call'd you pretty." — "Well, what then?
"I cannot hide my face from all the men;
"Alfred, indeed, indeed, you are deceived,
"He never spoke a word that I believed;
"Nay, can he think that I would leave a home
"Full of enjoyment, present, and to come,
"While your dear mother's favours daily prove
"How sweet the bonds of gratitude and love?
"No, while beneath her roof I shall remain,
"I'll never vex you, never give you pain."
"Enough, my life," he cried, and up they sprung;
By Heaven, I almost wish'd that I was young;
It was a dainty sight to see them pass,
Light as the July fawns upon the grass,
Pure as the breath of spring when forth it spreads,
Love in their hearts, and sunshine on their heads.

Next day I felt what I was bound to do,
To weigh the adventure well, and tell it too;
For Alfred's mother must not be beguiled,
He was her earthly hope, her only child;
I had no wish, no right to pass it by,
It might bring grief, perhaps calamity.
She was the judge, and she alone should know
Whether to check the flame or let it grow.
I went with fluttering heart, and moisten'd eye,
But strong in truth, and arm'd for her reply.

"Well, master Bowman, why that serious face?"
Exclaim'd the lovely dame, with such a grace,
That had I knelt before her, I had been
Not quite the simplest votary ever seen.
I told my tale, and urged that well-known truth,
That the soft passion in the bloom of youth

Starts into power, and leads th' unconscious heart
A chase where reason takes but little part;
Nothing was more in nature, or more pure,
And from their habits nothing was more sure.
Whether the lady blush'd from pride or joy,
I could but guess;—at length she said—"My boy
Dropp'd not a syllable of this to me!
What was I doing, that I could not see?
Through all the anxious hours that I have known,
His welfare still was dearer than my own;
How have I mourn'd o'er his unhappy fate!
Blind as he is! the heir to my estate!
I now might break his heart, and Jennet's too;
What must I, Bowman, or what can I do?"—
"Do, madam?" said I, boldly, "if you trace
"Impending degradation or disgrace
"In this attachment, let us not delay;
"Send my girl home, and check it while you may."
"I will," she said, but the next moment sigh'd;
Parental love was struggling hard with pride.

I left her thus, deep musing, and soon found
My daughter, for I traced her by the sound
Of Alfred's flageolet; no cares had they,
But in the garden bower spent half the day.
By starts he sung, then wildest trillings made,
To mock a piping blackbird in the glade.
I turn'd a corner and approach'd the pair;
My little rogue had roses in her hair!
She whipp'd them out, and with a downcast look,
Conquer'd a laugh by poring on her book.
My object was to talk with her aside,
But at the sight my resolution died;
They look'd so happy in their blameless glee,
That, as I found them, I e'en let them be;
Though Jennet promised a few social hours
'Midst her old friends, my poultry, and my flowers.
She came,—but not till fatal news had wrung

Her heart through sleepless hours, and chain'd her tongue.
She came, but with a look that gave me pain,
For, though bright sunbeams sparkled after rain,
Though every brood came round, half run, half fly,
I knew her anguish by her alter'd eye;
And strove, with all my power, where'er she came,
To soothe her grief, yet gave it not a name.
At length a few sad bitter tears she shed.
And on both hands reclined her aching head.
'Twas then my time the conqueror to prove,
I summon'd all my rhetoric, all my love.
"Jennet, you must not think to pass through life
"Without its sorrows, and without its strife;
"Good, dutiful, and worthy, as you are,
"You must have griefs, and you must learn to bear."
Thus I went on, trite moral truths to string, —
All chaff, mere chaff, where love has spread his wing:
She cared not, listen'd not, nor seem'd to know
What was my aim, but wiped her burning brow,
Where sat more eloquence and living power
Than language could embody in an hour.
With soften'd tone I mention'd Alfred's name,
His wealth, our poverty, and that sad blame
Which would have weigh'd me down, had I not told
The secret which I dare not keep for gold,
Of Alfred's love, o'erheard the other morn.
The gardener, and the woodbine, and the thorn;
And added, "Though the lady sends you home,
"You are but young, child, and a day may come" —
"She has *not* sent me home," the girl replied,
And rose with sobs of passion from my side;
"She has *not* sent me home, dear father, no;
"She gives me leave to tarry or to go;
"She has not *blamed* me, — yet she weeps no less,
"And every tear but adds to my distress;
"I am the cause, — thus all that she has done
"Will bring the death or misery of her son.
"Jealous he might be, could he but have seen
"How other lads approach'd where I have been;

"But this man's voice offends his very soul,
"That strange antipathy brooks no control;
"And should I leave him now, or seem unkind,
"The thought would surely wreck his noble mind;
"To leave him thus, and in his utmost need!
"Poor Alfred! then you will be blind indeed!
"I will not leave him."—"Nay, child, do not rave,
"What, would you be his menial, be his slave?"
"Yes," she exclaim'd, and wiped each streaming eye,
"Yes, be his slave, and serve him till I die;
"He is too just to act the tyrant's part,
"He's truth itself." O how my burthen'd heart
Sigh'd for relief!—soon that relief was found;
Without one word we traced the meadow round,
Her feverish hand in mine, and weigh'd the case,
Nor dared to look each other in the face;
Till, with a sudden stop, as if from fear,
I roused her sinking spirit, "Who comes here?"

Down the green slope before us, glowing warm,
Came Alfred, tugging at his mother's arm;
Willing she seem'd, but he still led the way,
She had not walk'd so fast for many a day;
His hand was lifted, and his brow was bare,
For now no clust'ring ringlets wanton'd there,
He threw them back in anger and in spleen,
And shouted "Jennet" o'er the daisied green.
Boyish impatience strove with manly grace
In ev'ry line and feature of his face;
His claim appear'd resistless as his choice,
And when he caught the sound of Jennet's voice,
And when with spotless soul he clasp'd the maid,
My heart exulted while my breath was staid.
"Jennet, we must not part! return again;
"What have I done to merit all this pain?
"Dear mother, share my fortune with the poor,
"Jennet is mine, and *shall* be—say no more;
"Bowman, you know not what a friend I'll be;

"Give me your daughter, Bowman, give her me;
"Jennet, what will my days be if you go?
"A dreary darkness, and a life of woe:
"My dearest love, come *home*, and do not cry;
"You are my daylight, Jennet, I shall die."

To such appeals all prompt replies are cold,
And stately prudence snaps her cobweb hold.
Had the good widow tried, or wish'd to speak,
This was a bond she could not, dared not break;
Their hearts (you never saw their likeness, never)
Were join'd, indissolubly join'd for ever.
Why need I tell how soon our tears were dried.
How Jennet blush'd, how Alfred with a stride
Bore off his prize, and fancied every charm,
And clipp'd against his ribs her trembling arm;
How mute we seniors stood, our power all gone?
Completely conquer'd, Love the day had won,
And the young vagrant triumph'd in our plight,
And shook his roguish plumes, and laugh'd outright.
Yet, by my life and hopes, I would not part
With this sweet recollection from my heart;
I would not now forget that tender scene
To wear a crown, or make my girl a queen.
Why need be told how pass'd the months along,
How sped the summer's walk, the winter's song,
How the foil'd suitor all his hopes gave up,
How Providence with rapture fill'd their cup?
No dark regrets, no tragic scenes to prove,
The gardener was too old to die for love.
A thousand incidents I cast aside
To tell but one—I gave away the bride—
Gave the dear youth what kings could not have given;
Then bless'd them both, and put my trust in Heaven.
There the old neighbours laugh'd the night away,
Who talk of Jennet's wedding to this day.
And could you but have seen the modest grace,
The half-hid smiles that play'd in Jennet's face,

Or mark'd the bridegroom's bounding heart o'erflow,
You might have wept for joy, as I could now:
I speak from memory of days long past;
Though 'tis a father's tale, I've done at last.

        * * * * *

Here rest thee, rest thee, Muse, review the scene
Where thou with me from peep of dawn hast been:
We did not promise that this motley throng
Should every *one* supply a votive song;
Nor every tenant: — yet thou hast been kind,
For untold tales must still remain behind,
Which might o'er listening patience still prevail.
Did fancy waver not, nor daylight fail.
"The Soldier's Wife," her toils, his battles o'er,
"Love in a Shower," the riv'let's sudden roar;
Then, "Lines to Aggravation" form the close,
Parent of murders, and the worst of woes.
But while the changeful hours of daylight flew,
Some homeward look'd, and talk'd of evening dew;
Some watch'd the sun's decline, and stroll'd around,
Some wish'd another dance, and partners found;
When in an instant every eye was drawn
To one bright object on the upper lawn;
A fair procession from the mansion came,
Unknown its purport, and unknown its aim.
No gazer could refrain, no tongue could cease,
It seem'd an embassy of love and peace.
Nearer and nearer still approach'd the train,
Age in the van transform'd to youth again.
Sir Ambrose gazed, and scarce believed his eyes;
'Twas magic, memory, love, and blank surprise,
For there his venerable lady wore
The very dress which, sixty years before,
Had sparkled on her sunshine bridal morn,
Had sparkled, ay, beneath this very thorn!
Her hair was snowy white, o'er which was seen,
Emblem of what her bridal cheeks had been,

A twin red rose — no other ornament
Had pride suggested, or false feeling lent;
She came to grace the triumph of her lord,
And pay him honours at his festive board.

Nine ruddy lasses follow'd where she stepp'd;
White were their virgin robes, that lightly swept
The downy grass; in every laughing eye
Cupid had skulk'd, and written "victory."
What heart on earth its homage could refuse?
Each tripp'd, unconsciously, a blushing Muse.
A slender chaplet of fresh blossoms bound
Their clustering ringlets in a magic round.
And, as they slowly moved across the green,
Each in her beauty seem'd a May-day queen.
The first a wreath bore in her outstretch'd hand,
The rest a single rose upon a wand;
Their steps were measured to that grassy throne
Where, watching them, Sir Ambrose sat alone.
They stopp'd, — when she, the foremost of the row,
Curtsied, and placed the wreath upon his brow;
The rest, in order pacing by his bower,
In the loop'd wreath left each her single flower, —
Then stood aside. — What broke the scene's repose?
The whole assembly clapp'd their hands and rose.

The Muses charm'd them as they form'd a ring,
And look'd the very life and soul of Spring!
But still the white hair'd dame they view'd with pride,
Her love so perfect, and her truth so tried.
Oh, sweet it is to hear, to see, to name,
Unquench'd affection in the palsied frame —
To think upon the boundless raptures past,
And love, triumphant, conquering to the last!

Silenced by feeling, vanquish'd by his tears,
The host sprung up, nor felt the weight of years;

Yet utterance found not, though in virtue's cause,
But acclamations fill'd up nature's pause,
Till, by one last and vigorous essay,
His tide of feeling roll'd itself away;
The language of delight its bondage broke,
And many a warm heart bless'd him as he spoke.

"Neighbours and friends, by long experience proved,
"Pardon this weakness; I was too much moved:
"My dame, you see, can youth and age insnare,
"In vain I strove, 'twas more than I could bear, —
"Yet hear me, — though the tyrant passions strive,
"The words of truth, like leading stars, survive;
"I thank you all, but will accomplish more —
"Your verses shall not die as heretofore;
"Your local tales shall not be thrown away,
"Nor war remain the theme of every lay.
"Ours is an humbler task, that may release
"The high-wrought soul, and mould it into peace.
"These pastoral notes some victor's ear may fill,
"Breathed amidst blossoms, where the drum is still:
"I purpose then to send them forth to try
"The public patience, or its apathy.
"The world shall see them; why should I refrain?
"'Tis all the produce of my own domain.
"Farewell!" he said, then took his lady's arm,
On his shrunk hand her starting tears fell warm;
Again he turn'd to view the happy crowd,
And cried, "Good night, good night, good night," aloud,
"Health to you all! for see, the evening closes,"
Then march'd to rest, beneath his crown of roses.
"Happy old man! with feelings such as these,
"The seasons all can charm, and trifles please."
An instantaneous shout re-echoed round,
'Twas wine and gratitude inspired the sound:
Some joyous souls resumed the dance again,
The aged loiter'd o'er the homeward plain,
And scatter'd lovers rambled through the park,

And breathed their vows of honour in the dark;
Others a festal harmony preferr'd,
Still round the thorn the jovial song was heard;
Dance, rhymes, and fame, they scorn'd such things as these,
But drain'd the mouldy barrel to its lees,
As if 'twere worse than shame to want repose:
Nor was the lawn clear till the moon arose,
And on each turret pour'd a brilliant gleam
Of modest light, that trembled on the stream;
The owl awoke, but dared not yet complain,
And banish'd silence re-assumed her reign.

THE END.